Red Light, Green Light

Red Light, Green Light

written by **Anastasia Suen**

illustrated by **Ken Wilson-Max**

Gulliver Books • Harcourt, Inc.

Orlando   Austin   New York   San Diego   Toronto   London

For my two new drivers; it feels like just minutes
ago that you were driving toy cars — A. C. S.

To Edgar Watson — K. W. M.

Text copyright © 2005 by Anastasia Suen
Illustrations copyright © 2005 by Ken Wilson-Max

www.HarcourtBooks.com

Gulliver Books is a trademark of Harcourt, Inc., registered in the United States
of America and/or other jurisdictions.

Library of Congress Cataloging-in-Publication Data
Suen, Anastasia.
Red light, green light/by Anastasia Suen; illustrated by Ken Wilson-Max.
p. cm.
"Gulliver Books."
Summary: A young boy creates an imaginary world filled with zooming cars,
flashing traffic lights, and racing fire engines.
[1. Transportation—Fiction. 2. Motor vehicles—Fiction. 3. Traffic signs and
signals—Fiction. 4. Stories in rhyme.] I. Wilson-Max, Ken, ill. II. Title.
PZ8.3.S9354Re 2005
[E]—dc22 2004017664
ISBN 0-15-202582-0

First edition
H G F E D C B A

Manufactured in China

The illustrations in this book were done in acrylic on paper.
The display type was set in Handy Sans and Bokka.
Color separations by Bright Arts Ltd., Hong Kong
Manufactured by South China Printing Company, Ltd., China
This book was printed on totally chlorine-free Stora Enso Matte paper.
Production supervision by Ginger Boyer
Designed by Scott Piehl and Jessica Dacher

Red light, stop.
Green light, go.

Cars and trucks
drive to and fro.

Big ones, small ones,
fat ones, thin...

driving out,
driving in.

Red lights flash.
Rail cars roll.

At the booth,
pay a toll.

Up above,
the choppers fly.

Traffic news
comes from the sky.

Now turn and turn
and turn some more.

Buses, trolleys
hurry past.

Fire engines
going fast!

Uptown, downtown, people know...

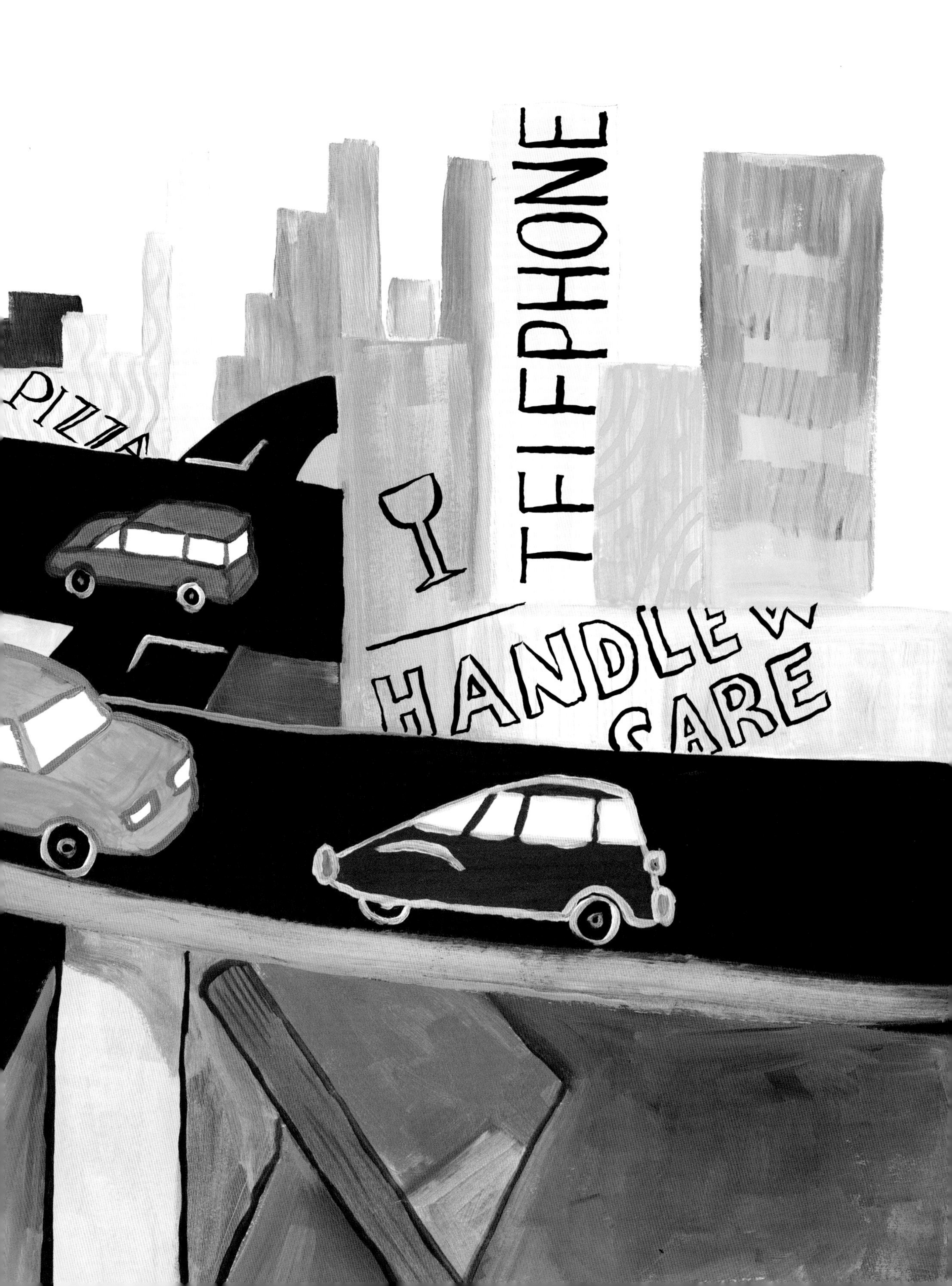
PIZZA
TELEPHONE
HANDLE W

Red light, stop.
Green light, go!